T0130563

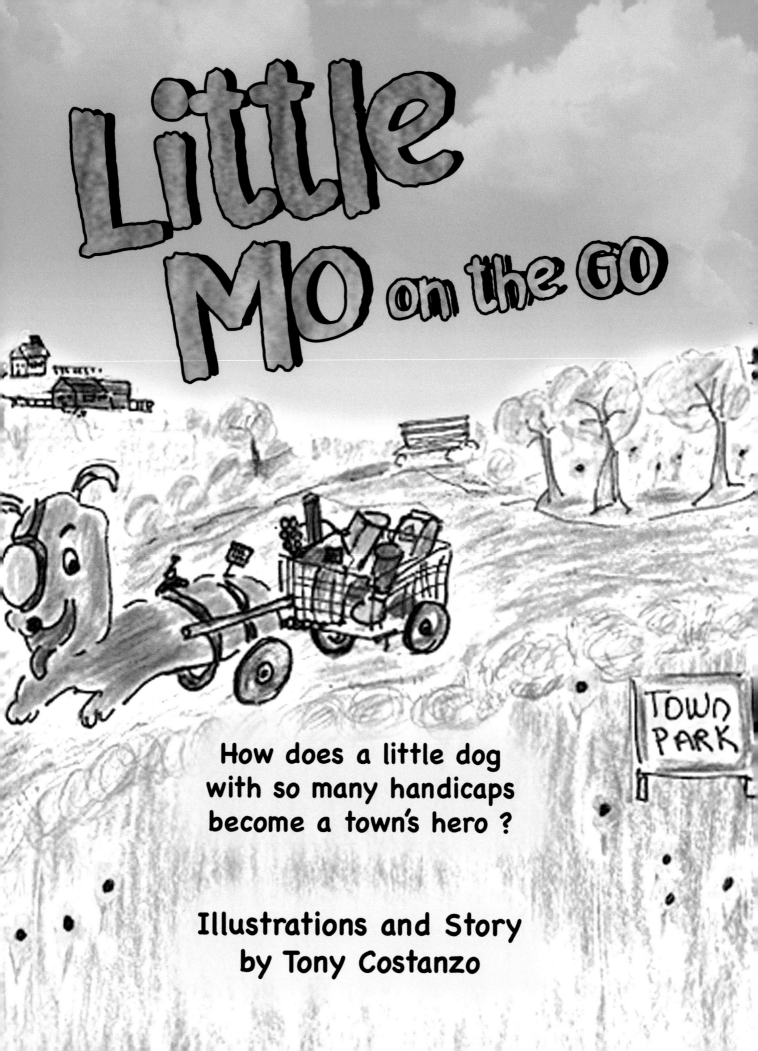

Little Mo on the GO

How does a little dog with so many handicaps become a town's hero?

Illustrations and Story by Tony Costanzo

Author and Book

My name is Tony Costanzo. I am a retired school teacher. I live in a small NH town bordering the Atlantic Ocean. My wife and I have been married for 52 years. We have two sons and a daughter. We also have a daughter in law, son in law, and two grandchildren.

This is a story of a small handicapped dog named Little Mo. A kind hearted inventor adopted him, giving him a chance at a better life.

I was inspired to write this story when I realized that animals can adjust to any handicaps they might have in amazing ways. Little Mo had to overcome a lot to survive. We all have to learn to live with some of life's hardships.

To order additional copies of this book, contact:
Xlibris
844-714-8691
www.Xlibris.com
Orders@Xlibris.com

ISBN: 978-1-6641-8437-4 (sc)
ISBN: 978-1-6641-8438-1 (hc)
ISBN: 978-1-6641-8436-7 (e)

Print information available on the last page

Rev. date: 07/22/2021

A Second Chance to Live

This is an incredible story about a tiny dog named Little Mo. He had everything against him coming into this world. He could hardly see out of one eye and was born without back legs. His little jaw wouldn't open completely to chew food. The doctors at the Animal Hospital tried everything. They were ready to give up on Little Mo. One of the hospital's doctors called his good friend, a scientist and inventor named Professor Chumly. "We have a tiny dog here that we named Little Mo, who has many serious problems", said the doctor. "I think that you are the only one who can help him. "Could you please come down to the animal hospital and take a look? "he begged. The kind hearted professor agreed and carefully took the helpless little dog home. "What good are all my inventions, If I can't use them to save a life", he thought to himself.

The professor's home was one big science experiment. Strange looking inventions and computers were everywhere. Somehow Professor Chumly had to design some devices to help this little dog survive. He thought back on a time when he had to design special glasses for his almost blind pet mouse, Freddy. Now, after a lot of training, Little Freddy had become like an assistant to him. Little Mo now had a second chance to live a full life. So much work and planning had to be done.

An Inventor Works Long Hours

This was the best thing that ever happened to Little Mo. Those first weeks went by very slowly. Mo slept on a soft cushion basket most of the time. The professor after many hours of hard work was able to design some clever inventions. The plan was to help Mo move since he had no back legs. The professor's pet mouse, Freddy, was a huge help. He put together all the tiniest gadgets and parts.

A giant computer screen helped the Professor, as he carefully put together everything. A binocular eye piece would be placed over that bad eye. It would enlarge objects, so Mo could see better. A set of wheels made of light aluminum with leather straps would be used for the back legs. Attached to the back would also be a light aluminum mini trailer. This way Mo could carry things and maybe even run errands. The professor then planned to connect a small solar panel computer to Mo's back which had a GPS tracker. It was like having a computer map of the town. All this so that Little Mo wouldn't get lost.

The plan was to slowly let Little Mo try these. He could practice in the back yard. The tiny dog needed to build up some strength. There was a big fence all around the yard to make it safe.

All Those Parts to Put Together

Professor Chumly has a creative imagination. He also uses his computer designs to help. He has to also make sure all this equipment wasn't too heavy for a small dog. Remember Mo was born with no back legs. All his pulling would be done by the front legs. The professor also designed a special one-piece eye glass to help Mo see better. Little Mo was almost blind in the right eye.

Freddy, the mouse, was a big help calming Mo down. The professor also taught Freddy how to use a small computer that added up numbers when he measured things. Freddy then recorded all the data for the professor. They were hoping that Little Mo could tow that light basket style trailer. This could be used to run errands or even pick up some groceries. The professor knew that turning the trailer around and backing up would not be easy.

Professor Chumly was a kind man. Little Mo always felt safe when he heard him talk in a gentle voice. "Don't worry," said the professor, "After a time, all these little parts wouldn't bother you." It did seem like so much stuff around him. If it helped Mo get around and do things, then it was worth it. Little Mo would have his freedom, almost like a regular dog.

Glow in the DARK Solar shoes

GREAT INVENTIONS OR JUST JUNK

When you looked around and saw how the professor lived you would say, "What is that crazy looking thing over there?" It was hard to tell the difference between a great invention or just plain junk. In the corner was what looked like a refrigerator and microwave all in one. It had buttons that made the frozen food go directly into the microwave above it. You could choose a frozen meal and have it cooked in the same appliance.

Freddy, his pet mouse, had his own tiny computer. The professor has a strange looking tree inside a plastic bubble. It grew grapes, apples, bananas, oranges and lemons. Believe it or not, they all grew from the same plant. Professor Chumly also has small plants watching TV. "I really think that plants are special," he said to Freddy. "They grow, drink water, like music, need air and sunlight," he went on to say. The professor's dream was to someday communicate with them.

On his desk was a solar hat with a small umbrella. Near the window was a space telescope. He like to look at the planets and International Space Station as it passed by. Today he was working on a special research project called Finger Print Money. You could pay for things with your finger prints. Then it's special ink would disappear, so that no one else could use it. He was an amazing inventor.

ALIENS FROM SPACE

The first week is a nightmare

One thing we have to understand was that Little Mo wasn't even a year old. So many things were new to him. His sense of hearing, smell and touching objects was all just starting. Living in an inventor's house could be a lot of fun for me and you, but they were very different for Little Mo. The first time he saw himself in the mirror he was shocked and frightened. He always went past the goldfish bowl real fast because the mean fish would squirt him with water. At the end of the work day, Professor Chumly always ran his vacuum to clean up his messes. Poor Mo stayed under a table the whole time shaking with fear, because it's loud motor sound and crackly noises.

After supper, the professor and Freddy sat back to relax and watch their favorite Outer Space Show on television. There hiding under the table was poor frightened Little Mo. Professor Chummly said, "Freddy, I don't know what we are going to do?" Freddy even tried to give Little Mo some of his popcorn. Mo wouldn't look up, as long as the space creature's faces were on the TV screen. The first week was not easy. Little Mo had a lot to learn. The professor had to come up with a better plan.

IZABELLA the CAT

Little Mo had been improving each week. The little dog could enjoy the protected back yard. Professor Chumly watched when he could from inside the house, but he was always very busy working on his inventions. The professor was so happy each day to see the amount of food Little Mo had eaten. The big dog tray was licked empty at the end of every day. "Wow, for such a little dog, he has a big appetite ", the Professor would say.

Then one day there was a shocking surprise. As the professor looked out the window he saw Isabella, the neighbor's big cat, in the yard. She must have somehow squeezed through a hole in the fence There she was gulping down all the food in Mo's tray, enjoying a free meal. Poor Little Mo looked scared and just watched from a distance. Isabella was almost three times bigger than Little Mo. She would just stare at him between gulps with her big green eyes. That scary look froze poor Little Mo. This is exactly what Professor Chumly feared the most. Little Mo would be pushed around and bullied by everyone. His small size and all his handicaps would work against him. The little dog had to learn to stand up for himself. He had to learn that he was important too!

Confusion Downtown

Mo was slowly improving. He was getting used to all that equipment, even those bumpy back wheels. Once a week Professor Chumly would order food from the market. "You won't get lost, just let the tracking device guide you", said the professor

Little Mo nervously went across town with his wagon. The tracking system would give Mo commands, so he knew where to go. The professor, however, never realized what other problems Mo faced as he bounced along the busy downtown sidewalks. Traffic lights, stop signs and town's people, would all be a big confusing mess. Mo did look clumsy with all those devices. On his way home, he was fooled by a downtown traffic light. Mo was late trying to cross at the busy crosswalk. A rude lady with two poodle dogs headed at him. She did not share any space and totally ignored Little Mo forcing him off the crosswalk. A large trash truck jammed on it's squeaky brakes. The driver yelled, "What's wrong with you, can't you see the red light?" It really frightened Mo. No one yelled at that lady.

Little Mo was really feeling down as he headed back with the supplies. Inside he felt hurt, nervous and upset. He was still very young and just didn't understand such things. He just had no confidence in himself. Mo didn't want to disappoint Professor Chumly when he got back home. "I'll try to act normal and pretend nothing happened," he thought to himself.

Sometimes Life is "No Walk in the Park"

Of course Professor Chumly could not control how people would treat Little Mo. It's sad that just because you look different, it can get you laughed at.

One of Little Mo's favorite places was the town's dog park. He could smell fresh air, feel sunlight and sniff the ground. He could look for scents down the trails like a regular dog. Mo had to work extra hard to pull those back wheels down the bumpy pathways. The solar panel on his back tracker sometimes twisted out of place. Sadly, however, people stared at him and pointed as Mo went by. He did appear kind of awkward with all that equipment. Sometimes he would even hear grownups tell their children to look the other way. A girl yelled to her mother, "Mummy what's wrong with that dog?" The mother answered, "Stay next to me." This really hurt the little dog's feelings. Maybe it was a blessing that he didn't see and hear too well.

Little Mo had a lot to learn about life. He didn't have much faith in himself. So many things made him fearful and nervous. Still he wanted to prove to Professor Chumly that he could at least do these errands with the cart.

Spike and His Gang

The town park was once crowded with families having picnics. Kids would ride their bikes there after school. You could fly kites and feed the birds. People use to go for walks. Joggers enjoyed a run on it's long trails. Others liked to sit on it's benches reading a book. All this changed when Spike and his gang of dogs took over. Spike had a sad life. He was abandoned by his owner when he was a puppy and just left outside an animal shelter. It was on a long holiday weekend, so that shelter was closed. After the owner drove off, Spike scampered away into the woods. Weeks later he ended up at the park where all this trouble started. He sort of took over the park, making it his own territory.

Many trails in the park could be dangerous. Spike and his dog gang could show up anytime. They growled and barked at anyone who came into their territory. They chased joggers and bike riders. Large holes were dug that ruined the trails. Families were just afraid to walk in the park.

Big Gus, the animal control officer, dreamed of the day when he could throw a net over Spike. He would be the town hero, collect the reward, and lock up Spike forever. Still nothing happened and the town's people were getting angry. Why was it taking so long to capture Spike?

Oh, no, Little Mo Is Surrounded

About a week later Little Mo was returning home from the market towing the weekly food support.

He cut through the park heading towards town; As Mo turned the corner, he sensed that he must have taken the wrong trail. "Things looked different, he thought to himself. Then everything happened so fast. Suddenly there were scary growling noises and the sound of scratching paws on the dirt. The dog pack, led by Spike, had easily surrounded defenseless Little Mo. They looked like a bunch of hungry seagulls circling a box of French fries left open on a beach blanket. All that loud barking scared Little Mo.

Amazingly the dogs were not interested in Little Mo. All eyes were on the loaded cart of treats. Spike could not stop drooling over the giant box of flavored dog biscuits. Mugzy's eyes opened two times wider as he looked at the candy fruit drops package. He could smell all the different flavors inside. Rhino had never seen a bag of chips before in his life. Would his giant teeth bite them one chip at a time?

Thankfully nobody paid any attention to a scared Little Mo. Not one dog noticed a certain dog catcher hiding in the bushes. Big Gus was watching all the action through his binoculars. He was zooming in on Spike. What was to happen next?

A Gift Wrapped Catch

Big Gus took one last look at Spike. He counted to himself, "three- two - one ". He stood up using all his power. He smashed the long net pole down over Spike's head. It banged down with such force, that part of the pole broke in his hand. The other dogs looked up at this giant of a man and scattered like a bunch of frightened chickens. The blow from the swinging net knocked out Spike. He was now gift wrapped perfectly for Big Gus to claim. They didn't nickname him Big Gus for nothing. He was clumsy and slow. Big Gus just couldn't move. His legs and one arm were locked tight by the thick brush. Those sharp needles had dug into his uniform. He was about to make the catch of his life, but he was caught too.

The scattering of the dogs made a dust cloud everywhere. This confused poor Little Mo. Then out of his one good eye, he saw Spike trapped inside the heavy net. On the ground was someone in a dog catcher's uniform tangled up in thick brush. Mo knew that he was in danger. He had to get out of there fast. He dug in with his front legs and off he went down the path. He was pulling the cart with a prisoner Spike inside. Big Gus could only watch.

Little Mo had to stay on the bumpy park trail and pass through town. He had to make it home. He found the strength and courage to keep going. Professor Chumly was the only one who could help him now.

Little Mo's Downtown Parade

It was the most surprising sight of all. Little Mo had made it to Main Street, downtown. He was covered with trail dust. His equipment was all twisted and bent. In his supply cart he was towing the town's most wanted law breaker, SPIKE. I mean Public Enemy Number One, the villain, the one who ruined their park, was finally captured. Spike still remained knocked out by the blow from the swinging metal handle. He was bleeding from the left ear. He was jammed tight inside a big net. Mo's front paws were badly scratched from the bushes. The tired little dog was now going even slower than normal. More people started to notice him.

The entire town became alive with excitement. People came out of stores and lined the sidewalks. Somebody shouted, "Hey look, he captured Spike!" The owner of the music store blasted parade sounds on his speakers. Everyone was cheering and taking pictures. A man said," Let's make the town park's name, Little Mo Park." This was Little Mo's victory parade. In a way his quick thinking also saved Spike from being sent away or even destroyed. Little Mo had the courage to pull that heavy cart away from danger. He had made it all the way to town. Now he had to make it home to Professor Chumly. He had to find the strength to keep going. He knew Spike would wake up soon.

There's No Place Like Home

Finally Little Mo pulled into his home driveway. Within minutes the Professor was next to him "You are a mess!" he said. Then came the biggest shock of all. As he looked through the netting, "This is Spike," he shouted, "How in the world did you capture him?" He bandaged up Little Mo who was all banged up. Next he helped Spike who was bleeding from the ear and still motionless.

Suddenly there was a bulletin on TV. "Breaking News, Spike, the town's most wanted fugitive, has been captured. It told of Mo's downtown parade with all the people cheering. What a story! The park would now be safe.

He made Mo rest and now helped Spike. He listened to Spike's sad story of how he was abandoned by a mean owner. He had to live on his own and hated people. Taking over the park was his way of getting even. You could see that Spike felt better around Professor Chumly. The Professor made a deal with Spike. "If you go to Dog Obedience School I will adopt you and take care of you." A happy Spike put his paw prints on the agreement.

One time Little Mo was given a second chance at life. Now he had given Spike a second chance. Spike would avoid being locked up forever.

Little Mo .... Special Mo

The next day, outside the house, more of town's people started to gather. They were all so happy to see their new hero, Little Mo. All the kids wanted their picture taken with him. Mo couldn't have been more excited. The officer put a special necklace around him, as a gift for his bravery. Spike was locked in the Dog Obedience School Van. He looked through the screen door towards Mo. He thought to himself, how things would have been so much worse, if it wasn't for Little Mo. He now had his second chance to live a good life.

Many of the town's people also now realized how mean they were too Little Mo. Somebody once said that you can't judge another living thing by only looking from the outside. You must close your eyes and open your heart to see the goodness and beauty inside. Acts of kindness always come back to you, and make you feel good, too. Little Mo felt so important. Professor Chumly was so proud of him. It wasn't just because of the medal around his neck.

LITTLE MO NOW KNEW, THAT THE INSIDE POWER HE HAD, FINALLY SHINED THROUGH!

Printed in the United States
by Baker & Taylor Publisher Services